For Anna-Katerina

Copyright © 2000 by Julie Lacome

All rights reserved.

First U.S. edition 2000

Library of Congress Cataloging-in-Publication Data

Lacome, Julie.
Ruthie's big old coat / Julie Lacome.–1st U.S. ed.
p. cm
Summary: Having been given a hand-me-down coat that is much too big,
Ruthie the rabbit finds that it is the perfect thing for her and her friend Fiona
to wear, and play in, together.
ISBN 0-7636-0969-2

[1. Coats–Fiction. 2. Play–Fiction. 3. Rabbits–Fiction.] 1. Title.
PZ7.L1357Ru 2000
[E]–dc21 99-28785

2 4 6 8 10 9 7 5 3 1

Printed in Hong Kong

This book was typeset in Humana and Providence.
The illustrations were done in acrylic and gouache.

Candlewick Press
2067 Massachusetts Avenue
Cambridge, Massachusetts 02140

RUTHIE'S BIG OLD COAT

JULIE LACOME

CANDLEWICK PRESS
CAMBRIDGE, MASSACHUSETTS

The coat used to belong
to Ruthie's cousin Frances.
Now it was Ruthie's turn
to wear it.

"This big old coat is too big,"
said Ruthie.
"You'll grow into it,"
said Mommy.

Ruthie tried to grow. Nothing happened.

Ruthie marched outside.
"This big old coat is
too big," she said.
Her friend Fiona
from next door
giggled.

"It *is* big," said Fiona. "It's big enough for me, too!"
She scooted inside and zipped it up.

Ruthie and Fiona
did the tango,
the twist,
and the
four-legged
turkey trot.

They played Monster,

Big Red
Air Balloon,

and DANGER Poisonous Mushroom.

They zoomed across the garden on Fiona's skateboard.

Ruthie looked at Fiona
in the big old coat.

Fiona looked at Ruthie
in the big old coat.

They got a big case of the Big Old Coat Giggles.

All of a sudden, Ruthie stopped laughing.
All of a sudden, Ruthie needed to
go to the bathroom.

Fiona tugged and tugged, but the zipper
was stuck!

"The zipper won't unstick, it won't, it won't,"
cried Fiona.

"Forget the zipper," said Ruthie. "I've got to go NOW!"

"Zoinks!" yelled Fiona. "Let's run for it!"

Fiona said she wouldn't look and Ruthie scrunched her pants down and…

"Oh, Ruthie," Mommy said
as she unstuck the zipper.
"This coat really is
too big and too old."

"Oh, Mommy," said Ruthie, giving her a kiss, "we love this coat."
"Zoinks!" said Fiona. "It's perfect!"

The coat *was* perfect.
It was perfect for
Twin-Engine Airplane
Gone Loco…

and perfect for the biggest-ever case
of the Big Old Coat Giggles.